Text by Charlotte Evans Thomas
Illustrations by Deborah Jonsson
Production Design by Lu Ann Hammond Hirsch

Golden Rings Publishing Company
PO Box 25046
6173 Doe Haven Drive
Farmington, New York 14425

Printed in the United States of America

First Edition, 1992
10 9 8 7 6 5 4 3 2

ISBN 0-9633607-0-1
Library of Congress Catalog Card Number 92-72538

Summary: Our Little Flower Girl's apprehensions are reduced as she becomes involved in the
excitement of planning and participating in her aunt's wedding day.

Dedication

This book is dedicated to
my granddaughter,
Amanda Cay Thomas,
who brings joy to so many people,
and to all little girls everywhere
who dream of one day being a bride.

Mandy was splashing in the bathtub and singing happily. Her mom had called to her twice, but Mandy hadn't heard. So Mom poked her head into the bathroom and said, "Aunt Melody will be here soon. Please finish your bath and I'll fix your hair."

Mandy quickly put her toys on the edge of the tub and began drying herself with her big, fluffy clown towel. She had been having such a good time with her tub toys, she had forgotten that this was the day Aunt Melody was coming for lunch. Mom had told her it was to be a special day, and that Aunt Melody had a big surprise for Mandy.

Mandy's mom was tying the last hair ribbon into place as the doorbell rang. Mandy ran to the door, and there stood her favorite aunt with a big smile and open arms. She kissed Mandy and gave her what they both called "Baby Bear Hugs."

Aunt Melody held out her hand and showed Mandy a beautiful, sparkling diamond ring. She said, "Joe and I are getting married." Mandy was so happy she started jumping up and down. She loved Joe almost as much as she loved her daddy. Then Mom said, "Aunt Melody, don't you have another surprise for Mandy?"

Aunt Melody sat Mandy on her lap and told her, "Joe and I would like you to be part of our BIG DAY. We want our favorite little girl to lead the wedding party down the aisle. Will you please say yes, and be OUR LITTLE FLOWER GIRL?" Mandy opened her eyes real wide. "I want to say yes, but I'm a little scared. I don't know how to be a Flower Girl," she said. Aunt Melody smiled and explained, "Sweetie, you just have to look pretty, as you always do, and carry a colorful basket of flowers and petals to scatter as you walk."

Mandy shouted, "Yes, yes!" But then she started asking all kinds of questions. "When will it be? What will I wear? What do I have to do besides look pretty?" Mom and Aunt Melody laughed and told her that the wedding wouldn't be for a few months and she would learn everything she needed to know at a "rehearsal" the night before the BIG DAY. Then they told her the best news of all — that she would need a very special dress. One that would be fancier and prettier than any dress she had ever seen.

Mandy was so excited she had trouble eating her lunch. She kept thinking of more and more questions to ask. After Mandy finished her dessert, Mom said, "Let's go shopping and maybe we can get an idea what kind of dress Mandy could wear."

They all agreed it was a good day to get started. Aunt Melody suggested they go to The Bridal Shoppe where she had already bought her wedding gown. The saleslady greeted them at the door. Then she looked at Mandy. "So this is the lucky little girl you were telling me about," she said. "She must have said yes. I'm sure that made everyone happy."

"A dress came in this morning, and I could just picture it in your aunt's wedding." She went into another room and brought out the most beautiful dress Mandy had ever seen. After the saleslady made a few changes to make it fit properly, Mandy tried it on and she felt all grown-up.

As Mandy looked into the mirror, she could picture herself walking down the aisle, leading the wedding party. Everyone agreed it was the perfect dress. Then Mandy, admiring herself in the mirror all the time, said, "I can't wait to show Daddy tonight." The saleslady explained that the dress was a sample, just for trying on, but that she would order one that would fit perfectly, and it would take only a few weeks.

They decided, since they had found the dress so quickly, that it was a good day to buy the shoes and stockings and hair ribbons to go with it. In no time at all, they were able to find everything they needed to make Mandy's outfit complete.

The next morning, Mandy was anxious to go outside and play with her friends. She told them about her beautiful new dress, and that she was to be the Flower Girl in her aunt's wedding.

For the next few weeks their favorite game was playing "Getting Married." They used all of their dolls and stuffed animals as the bridal party. They made sure that everyone's toy got a turn at being the bride. Mandy's mom filled a little basket with flower petals so Mandy could practice scattering them.

Mandy and her mom met the rest of the bridal party at the church the night before the wedding for the rehearsal to practice Mandy's part, and make sure everything would be perfect. Most of Aunt Melody's girlfriends were bridesmaids. Her best friend was the maid of honor. Joe's closest friend was the best man, and his friends were ushers. Aunt Melody explained to Mandy that the maid of honor and best man are the ones who help the bride and groom the most. They all marched in and out to the music, so they would know just what to do. Mandy practiced walking very, very slowly and even practiced smiling so she wouldn't forget the next day.

After everyone was sure they knew exactly what to do, they went
out to have dinner at a nice restaurant. Mandy soon got sleepy and
her mom took her home to bed.

On the big day, Mandy looked out the window to see the sun shining brightly. She couldn't wait to put on her new dress. She ate breakfast and had her bath.

Mandy sang, but she didn't play with any toys because there was just
too much to do. When she was all dressed, her mom tied her hair
with the beautiful ribbons they had bought.

Mandy arrived at the church with her mom and dad just in time to
see Aunt Melody and Mandy's grandfather, whom everyone called
"Pop-Pop," drive up in a long white car. They hurried inside, and
Mandy went in right behind them.

The maid of honor handed Mandy a beautiful basket of flowers and flower petals with ribbons hanging from it. The bridesmaids were lining up while the organ played soft, pretty music. Everyone was trying to be quiet while they waited in the back of the church. Then the chimes struck two, meaning the long awaited time had finally arrived.

Mandy was the first one down the aisle, smiling and reaching into her basket for the flower petals. She scattered them on one side and then the other. She had remembered everything, including her bright, pretty smile, and was very proud of herself. She turned to watch Aunt Melody walking down the aisle holding Pop-Pop's arm, and saw that they, too, had big smiles.

Mandy stood up straight and still, as her mom and Aunt Melody
had told her. When she saw Aunt Melody and Joe kiss each other,
she knew it would soon be time to march out as they had practiced.

People took lots of pictures at the church. Mandy had never seen so many flashes going off at one time. After the wedding photographer was finished taking pictures of the bridal party, they went to a big room where a wonderful party was getting started. Mandy's mom told her the party was called a "reception."

Mandy felt very grown-up sitting with the wedding party at the big head table, and was very careful of her manners so Mom and Dad could be proud of her. There was lots of music, dancing and all kinds of fun. And best of all, there was a really big cake.

Pop-Pop and Mandy twirled around the dance floor. When they came close to Aunt Melody and Joe, they traded partners.

Joe danced with Mandy and whispered in her ear, "Mandy, you are the prettiest Flower Girl in the whole world." Mandy blushed, and whispered back to him, "I've never, ever had such a fun day." Joe promised to send her a picture postcard from the honeymoon trip he and Aunt Melody were taking the next day.

Mandy was a very tired and happy little girl when she got into bed that night, and she quickly fell fast asleep.

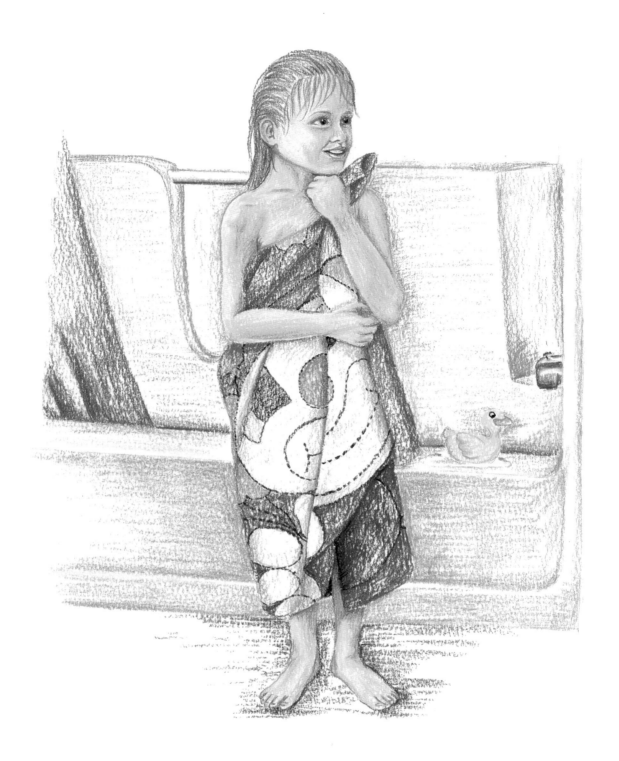

The next morning, when she was having her bath and once again singing all of her favorite songs, she added a few songs she had learned the night before. She splashed and played for a long, long time with all of her tub toys. When her mom came in with her big, fluffy clown towel, Mandy thought for a minute. Then she asked, "Mommy, how long will it be till I can be the bride?"

THE END

The Big Day

your photo here

Bridal Party Autographs

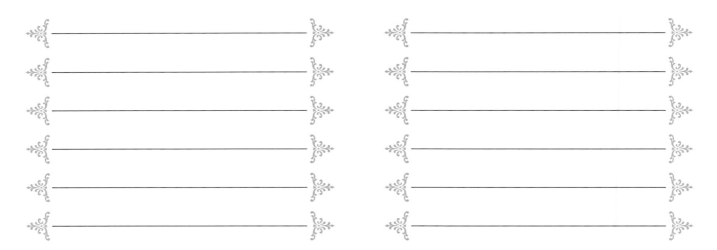

Special Friends